POKÉMON
ADVANCED ®
SNACK ATTACK!

READER

Adapted by Tracey West

Scholastic Inc.

New York   Toronto   London   Auckland   Sydney

Mexico City   New Delhi   Hong Kong   Buenos Aires

ISBN 0-439-55992-8

12 11 10 9 8 7 6 5   4 5 6 7 8 9/0
Printed in the U.S.A.
First printing, January 2004

Ash and Pikachu have two new friends.
May and her little brother Max joined their Pokémon journey.

They walked through the woods for a long time.

"Can we stop for lunch?" May asked. "I am so hungry!"

"No way!" said Max. "I want to find some Pokémon first."

"We can stop for a quick lunch," Ash said. "Then we will look for Pokémon."

"Yay!" said May and Max.

But there was a problem. All of their food was gone!

"Pika!" cried Pikachu.

Its can of Pokémon food was empty, too!

"I wish my old friend Brock was here," Ash said. "He knows a lot about Pokémon. And he knows a lot about cooking, too!"

Not far away, Team Rocket watched
the hungry friends.

Jessie, James, and Meowth were
always trying to steal Pikachu.

"Hey look," Meowth said.
"Something's happening!"

Max found a cookie in his pack.
A Pokémon swooped down before
Max could take a bite.
It stole the cookie and flew to a tree!

"A Taillow stole my cookie!" Max yelled.

Ash looked up the Taillow in his Pokédex.

"Taillow can be fierce," said the computer. "These flying Pokémon will not back down in a fight."

"Give us back that cookie!" May yelled.

"Wait," Ash said. "This tree is full of fruit. Pikachu, help us knock down some of that fruit."

Zap! Pikachu shocked the trees.
A flock of Taillow flew out!
"I think they are going to attack!"
Max cried.

"Pikachu , Thunderbolt!" Ash yelled.

Pikachu zapped the Taillow. They fell to the ground.

Then they got right back up!

The leader of the Taillow attacked
Pikachu.

PIkachu did its best. But it could not
beat the Taillow.

"Taillow are very fierce fighters," Ash
said.

The Taillow flock joined the attack.
Ash did not know what to do.
Suddenly, a Foretress joined the fight!

"Foretress, Explosion!" a voice cried. *Boom!* Smoke filled the woods. The Taillow flock flew away.

The smoke cleared. Ash saw his friend Brock standing there.

"Thanks, Brock," Ash said. "Your Foretress saved the day."

"Are you really a good cook?" May asked Brock. "Because we could use some lunch!"

"Sure," Brock said. He looked in his pack.

"My sandwiches are gone!" Brock cried.

"I bet the Taillow ate them," May said. "They ate our food, too."

"No problem," Brock said. "I can stir up some stew."

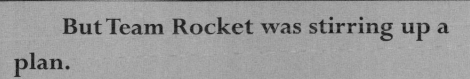

But Team Rocket was stirring up a plan.

"Let's get the Taillow to do our dirty work for us," Meowth said.

Team Rocket had
Brock's sandwiches.
They fed them to the
hungry Taillow.

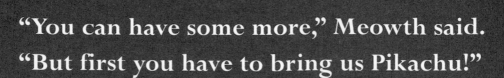

"You can have some more," Meowth said.
"But first you have to bring us Pikachu!"

The leader of the Taillow challenged Pikachu to a fight.
     Taillow and Pikachu faced off.

Zap! Pikachu shocked Taillow.

Swoop! Taillow flew down. It picked up Pikachu. Then it dropped Pikachu in the river!

"You have to end the battle," Brock told Ash. "Taillow will not back down."

Ash threw out a Poké Ball. A light zapped Taillow. The Poké Ball closed.

"I caught a Taillow!" Ash cried.

But the battle was not over. The rest of the Taillow flock wanted to fight Pikachu, too.

Ash's Taillow tried to talk them out of it.

"Give up, Taillow!" Meowth called.

"That is right," said Jessie. "These Taillow are our very own fierce fighting force!"

"They will do anything for sandwiches," added James.

"Hey!" May yelled. "*I wanted those sandwiches!*"

May threw out a Poké Ball. Torchic popped out.

But May forgot to give Torchic a command.

The little Fire Pokémon ran into a rock.

Jessie laughed. "Taillow, attack!"

The Taillow swooped down.

Ding! A bell rang.

"My stew is ready," Brock said.
"Come and get it, Taillow."

The Taillow stopped the attack. They ate the stew instead.

There was enough stew for everybody . . . except Team Rocket.

Pikachu sent them blasting off with a Thunder Shock.

Finally, the Taillow flock ate their fill.
They flew away.

Ash's Taillow said good-bye to its
friends.

Ash wanted to get moving, too. "Catching a Taillow was fun," Ash said. "Let's go look for more Pokémon!"

"Hold on, Ash," Brock said. "We have to do the dishes first."

Ash smiled. "It's good to have you back, Brock," he said.

"Friends should always stick together," said Brock.

"*Pika!*" agreed Pikachu.